Smartypantus Rulus O.K.us

First published in Great Britain by Hamish Hamilton
Children's Books in 1986
First published in Picture Lions 1988
10
Picture Lions is an imprint of the Children's Division,
part of HarperCollins Publishers Limited,
77-85 Fulham Palace Road, Hammersmith,
London W6 8JB

ISBN: 0 00 662798-6

Printed and bound in Hong Kong

PictureLions
An Imprint of HarperCollins*Publishers*

Princess SmartyPants

by

Babette Cole

Princess Smartypants did not want to get married.
She enjoyed being a Ms.

Because she was very pretty and rich, all the princes wanted her to be their Mrs.

Princess Smartypants wanted to live in her castle with her pets and do exactly as she pleased.

"It's high time you smartened yourself up,"
said her Mother the Queen.
"Stop messing about with those
animals and find yourself
a husband!"

uitors were always turning up at the castle
aking a nuisance of themselves.
ight," declared Princess Smartypants, "whoever can accomplish the
asks that I set will, as they say, win my hand."

She asked Prince Compost to stop
the slugs eating her
garden.

She asked
Prince Rushforth
to feed her pets.

e challenged
nce Pelvis to a
ler-disco marathon.

She invited Prince Boneshaker for a
cross-country ride on her motorbike.

She called on Prince Vertigo
to rescue her from her tower.

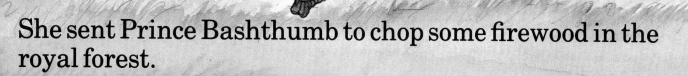

She sent Prince Bashthumb to chop some firewood in the royal forest.

She suggested to Prince Fetlock that he
might like to put her pony through its paces.

She told Prince Grovel to take her
Mother the Queen shopping.

She commanded Prince Swimbladder to retrieve her magic ring from the goldfish pond.

None of the princes could accomplish the task he was set. They all left in disgrace. "That's that then," said Smartypants, thinking she was safe.

Then Prince Swashbuckle
turned up.

He stopped the slugs eating her garden . . .

. . . fed her pets . . .

. . . roller-discoed
until dawn. . .

. . . rode for miles
on her motorbike . . .

He rescued her
from her tower.

He found some firewood to chop in the forest.

He even tamed her horrid pony . . .

. . . took her Mother the Queen shoppin

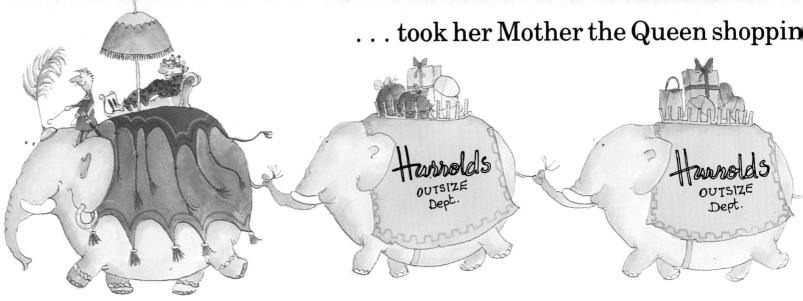

and retrieved her magic ring from the goldfish pond.

Prince Swashbuckle didn't think Princess Smartypants was so smart.

So she gave him a magic kiss . . .

. . . and he turned into a
gigantic warty toad!

Prince Swashbuckle left in a big hurry!

When the other princes heard what had happened to Prince Swashbuckle, none of them wanted to marry Smartypants . . .

. . . so she lived happ
ever aft